the LITTLE Cockroach

SUSIE VIOLET

illustration by Alex Patrick

Published by
Twinky & Hoobie Publishing

Copyright 2018 by Susie Violet
Published by Twinky & Hoobie Publishing
ISBN: 978-1-9993232-3-3

Illustrations by Alex Patrick

Creative and Print by SpiffingCovers Ltd.

To

Elsie & Henry

"Try and you might,
don't and you certainly won't!"

Pedro the Little Cockroach
was very **bored** one day,

as he looked across
the sand dunes
in sunny Angel Bay.

'I'm **tired** of this place,'
Pedro said to his best friend.

'There **must** be **more**
than sun and sand,
to make this _boredom_ end!'

He said, 'I know, Enrico!
We should go and
have some fun!'

They packed some shoes
and two canoes, and so
the adventure began!

They left the bay to find a way.
The road was unfriendly
and SCARY.

Watching out for predators,
they needed to be wary.

Prowling in the **shadows**
was a gecko's silhouette!
Pedro and Enrico upped their pace.
'We **NEED** to lose this threat!'

'Yippeeeee, we lost it,' Pedro said.
They danced around with glee.

Despite the close encounter,
they had never felt so free.

'LOOK, an airport,' Enrico cried.
And they ran towards the lights.
'Jump on this case,' Pedro said,
as they ZOOMED to catch a flight.

Through the airport they whizzed.
'HANG ON, Enrico! Hold tight!'
The roaches clasped with all their strength

with the **cargo** hold in **sight!**

Arrrrrrrrriba, away they flew,
high up into the sky.
The little bugs were on their way,
waving their home goodbye.

They arrived in a new land,
of spaghetti and old buildings!
'We made it, Pedro, we really did!
Here's to new **beginnings!**

'Where **ARE** we?' Enrico said.
'I'm not sure!' Pedro replied.
'Grab a camera; find your map,
and let's follow that tour guide!'

'Let's go or "Andiamo"
Is what the locals say.'
They walked up a wonky tower,
with Pedro leading the way.

They scuttled on through the crowds.
'Come over here!' Pedro said.
'OH NO, ENRICO, WATCH OUT!'
as ice-cream plopped on his head.

Sweet, sticky and smooth.
Licking up the goo.
The ice-cream melted,
with plenty for two.

They came across a kitchen, and disguised as **pepperoni,**

they were picked up by the chef, and **plonked** into a calzone!

Inside a pizza oven they sat.
It was toasty and yummy.

This was the best place to be,
and perfect for their tummies.

Unaware of the outside world,
the bugs tucked in with delight.
A knife came tearing through;
their delight turned into FRIGHT!

Screams echoed through the air
with people in a panic.

Pedro yelled, 'WE NEED TO LEAVE!
this atmosphere's too manic.'

After all the exploring
they decided to sleep.

All their whizzing
and whooshing
had quite worn out their feet.

They scurried into a grand hotel.
'Get in here,' Pedro said.
The little bugs found a case
to make the **perfect** bed!

They talked about the gecko,
and flying in the sky.

Their heads **buzzing** with
all they'd done, they started
to close their eyes.

Pedro started snoring,
Enrico snuggled in tight.
Tomorrow would be another adventure,
but for now they said 'Night-night!'

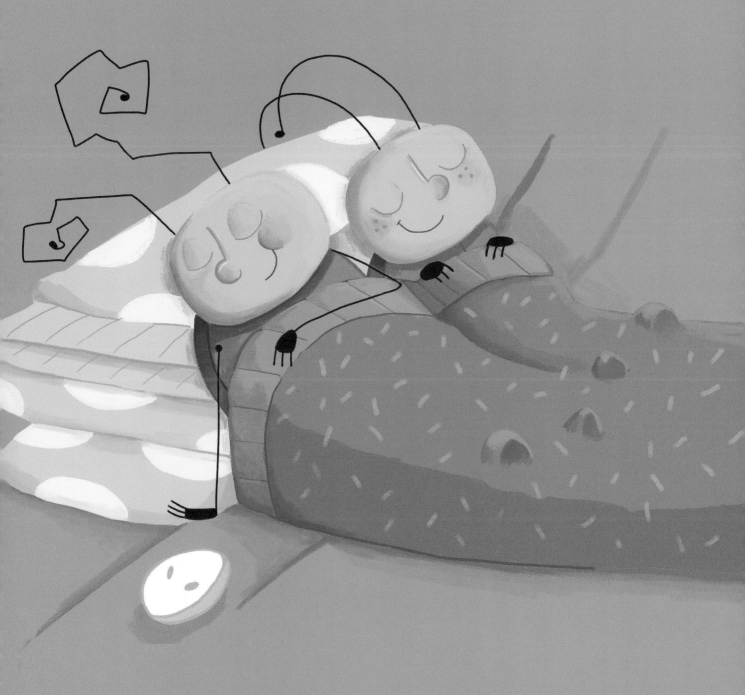

'Roach

Trip!

Thank you!

A very special thank you to my awesome husband **Robbie** who has offered endless support and bucket-loads of optimism.

Thank you to my **mum & dad** who made me believe I could do anything.

A huge thanks to **Victoria Lee** whose ongoing advice and encouragement was invaluable to me during my writing journey. Further thanks go to **Pippa Goodhart** for her initial critique and enthusiasm for the story.

And finally to all of St. Anne's KG2 class of 2017/18. It was their unanimous vote of confidence that gave me a boost to get this over the line.

Printed in Great Britain
by Amazon